Evie's Field Day

MORE THAN ONE WAY TO WIN

By Claire Annette Noland

Illustrated by Alicia Teba

Evie's Field Day: More Than one Way to Win

Summary: Evie wants more than anything to win the school's field day events, but when faced with a bird that needs help, she loses the race and discovers that there is more than one way to win.

Our books may be purchased in bulk for promotional, educational or business use. Please contact your local bookseller or IPG Books at orders@ipgbook.com

Library of Congress Control Number:2019942059
ISBN (hardcover): 978-1-7330359-0-3
ISBN (picture book): 978-1-7330359-1-0
ISBN (Ebook:) 978-1-7330359-2-7

The art in this book was created using digital pencil and watercolor made with photoshop

Book design by: Maggie Villaume

Cardinal Rule Press

5449 Sylvia
Dearborn Heights, MI 48125
Visit us at www.CardinalRulePress.com

BEFORE READING

- Read the title of the book.
- Ask your child if they know what a "Field Day" is.
- Discuss what kinds of games and sports they like to play.
- Ask your child how they feel when they win and when they lose.
- To develop empathy, ask them how they think the other person they are playing with feels when they lose.

WHILE READING

- The main character Evie has strong opinions on winning. What are they?
- What do you think Evie is feeling at Field Day?
- How does she feel when she doesn't win? How does she treat her friends? Is she happy for them?
- When Evie is finally ahead in the race, she makes a decision to help a baby bird, which causes her to lose the race. Ask your child to put his/herself in Evie's place. What would they do?

AFTER READING

- Have your child describe how Evie feels when the bird flies back to its mother.
- How do her friends react to Evie's act of kindness?
- Why do Evie's friends cheer for her when she crosses the finish line in last place?
- What does "there's more than one way to win" mean?

Make time to play games or to participate in low-key competitive activities with your child so they can develop strategies to deal with the disappoints that come with losing but also how to be a good winner. Put the emphasis on having fun because that's the best thing about playing together!

DEDICATED TO...

My family whose stories
provide endless inspiration.

– Claire Noland

Those who stand up and
fight for the weak.

– Alicia Teba

Evie loved to win.

She could jump the highest, run the fastest, and hop the farthest.

Evie had a special place in her room where she kept her trophies and ribbons.

So, on Field Day, Evie looked forward to adding to her collection.

Evie lined up behind her friends for the beanbag toss.

Zing!

Zing!

Zip!

Marty went first. *Zing, zing, zip.*

Two of his beanbags landed in the box.

Gloria was next. *Zing, zing, zing!*

Zing!

Zing!

Zing!

All three of her beanbags went in the box.

Then it was Evie's turn. She flung the first beanbag. *Zoom.* It went too far.

ZooOOOooom!

She tossed the second beanbag. *Zip.* It didn't go far enough.

Finally, she threw the third beanbag. *Zoop!* It hit the box and fell to the ground.

Gloria was the winner!

Everyone shouted, "Hooray!"

Except Evie.

Next, Evie skipped over to the musical hoops game.

She stood in a hoop and
smiled at Marty and Gloria.

She knew she could hop
the farthest.

The music started and everyone
hopped from hoop to hoop.

A hoop was taken away.

The music stopped and
everyone scrambled.

But there weren't enough hoops.

Gloria was out.

The music played again.
Everyone hopped from
hoop to hoop.

Every time the music stopped, someone was out.

Finally, only Marty and Evie were left.

They hopped and hopped. The music stopped.

There was only one hoop.

Marty won!

"Hooray!" everyone shouted.

Except Evie.

Splash!

Evie walked with a cup
of water on her head.

Splash!

She tussled in the balloon stomp. *Pop!*

Pop!

She even tried to run with an egg on a spoon.

Splat!

Splat!

Evie was worried.
She had not won anything.

It was time for Evie's favorite event - the sack race.

Evie got into a sack and lined up between Marty and Gloria.

She gave them a thumbs up.

She *knew* she was the best jumper.

She heard, "On your mark, get set, go!"

Evie jumped high,

Evie jumped fast.

Evie jumped far.

She was winning!

But then she saw a fluttering baby bird.

It landed right in the path of the racers.

Evie could jump over the little bird, but what if the others couldn't? Evie stopped.

She scooped up the bird as the other children jumped past her.

She held the bird up, and it flapped back to its mama.

Evie came in last.

She heard everyone shouting, *Hooray!*

Hooray!

Then she heard her name.

The children were shouting, "Hooray for Evie!"

Evie grinned.

Some things are better than winning.

10 SUGGESTIONS

to Help Your Children Learn Good Sportsmanship

Participating in games and competitions can help children learn important skills, such as cooperation, patience, and teamwork. Everyone likes to win but, in any competition, someone loses. Learning to navigate through the emotions that come with winning or losing is an important life skill. Here are some ways you can help your child learn good sportsmanship.

1. **Preparation.** Make sure your child understands the game before they start. Explain that there will be a winner and loser. Talk to them about how to play fair and put the emphasis on having fun.

2. **Identify and Control Emotions.** Children caught up in a game or activity can get upset when the outcome isn't what they wanted. Help them to develop strategies like taking a deep breath or walking away from the situation to calm down.

3. **Acknowledge their feelings.** It is disappointing to lose and often exhilarating to win but they need to know that their worth is not tied to winning or losing. Value comes from who they are and not from how they perform.

4. **Be a good friend.** Children need to learn to empathy. If someone gets hurt, is frustrated, or is sad about losing, help them develop ways to show their care and concern. Show them ways they can cheer their friends and teammates on.

5. **Be a good winner.** No one likes someone who boasts, brags, or makes fun of the loser. Help your child to acknowledge and thank their competitor.

6. **Be a gracious loser.** Yes, it's hard to lose, but help your child to be happy for the winner. Let them know that it is important to offer congratulations by giving a thumbs up or a high five. It's okay to lose, but not okay to blame others for the loss.

7. **Find people who display good sportsmanship.** When watching a sport or competition with your child, be on the lookout for people who are gracious in winning and losing. Find players who reach out and help others on opposing teams. Likewise, when you see people behaving badly, help your child to identify those traits. Discuss why some actions are or are not right.

8. **Give Praise.** Catch your child when they play fair and are kind to others. Focus on their positive attitude rather than on winning.

9. **Set goals.** With games and sports that require developing skills, emphasize the effort, not the outcome. The goal should be on improving and doing better rather than winning.

10. **Play together.** Find games and activities to play together that have a clear winner and loser like Bingo, Chutes and Ladders, and Candyland. Help your child to develop the vocabulary and gestures to use in different competitive situations by modeling them yourself. Good job!

Play Good Sport/Bad Sport

Help your child identify traits of good and bad sportsmanship by reading the following scenarios to your child: Have them give Thumbs Up for helpful behavior, and Thumbs Down for hurtful behavior.

- Gives a high five!
- Frowns and stomps feet.
- Says "I hate losing!"
- Says "Let's play again."
- Says "Hooray for me – I'm number one!"
- Says "Good job!"
- Says "No one can beat me!"
- Says "Can you show me how you did that?"

- Says "Congratulations!"
- Says "No fair, you cheated!"
- Says "Let me help you."
- Says "I'm not going to play with you anymore!"
- Gives a Thumbs Up
- Laughs at the person who lost
- Cheers when somebody does well

AUTHOR

Claire Annette Noland

Claire Annette Noland knows that everyone who reads is a winner. As a children's librarian, reading specialist, and author, she has made it her life's goal to get kids excited about books and reading.

Claire lives with her family on a river in central California. She has never won a sack race but she keeps trying.

Alicia Teba

Alicia was born in Spain. She has been drawing since she was three, and has never stopped. She studied cinema and arts. She has been working as an illustrator for known Spanish publishers and this is her fifth book. She also has done comics for magazines and stationary design.

She has always loved animals and nature and this is very apparent in her artwork.

ILLUSTRATOR

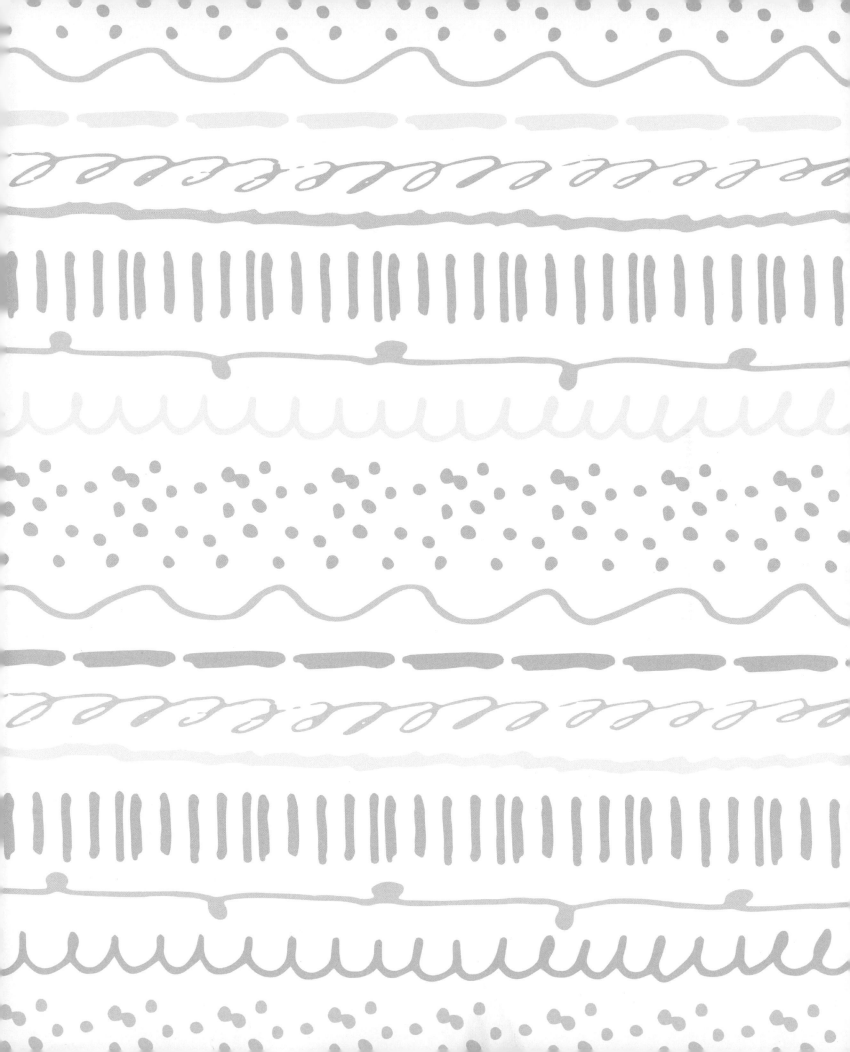